Don't Worry, MURRAY

David Ezra Stein

BALZER + BRAY
An Imprint of HarperCollinsPublishers

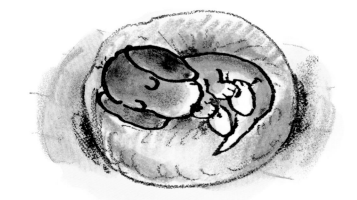

Balzer + Bray is an imprint of HarperCollins Publishers.

Don't Worry, Murray
Copyright © 2022 by David Ezra Stein
All rights reserved. Manufactured in Italy.
No part of this book may be used or reproduced in any manner whatsoever without written
permission except in the case of brief quotations embodied in critical articles and reviews.
For information address HarperCollins Children's Books, a division of HarperCollins
Publishers, 195 Broadway, New York, NY 10007.
www.harpercollinschildrens.com

Library of Congress Control Number: 2021936551
ISBN 978-0-06-284524-5

The artist used bamboo pen and ink, charcoal, graphite, watercolor,
crayon, and photocopy to create the illustrations for this book.
Typography by Dana Fritts
22 23 24 25 26   RTLO   10 9 8 7 6 5 4 3 2 1
❖
First Edition

To all the brave dogs out there,
who keep on putting one paw
in front of the other

Good morning, Murray!

Why don't you want to go outside, Murray?

Don't worry, Murray!
You can wear your raincoat.

Good boy, Murray! Good boy.

Murray?

Why don't you want to say hello
to this new dog, Murray?

Don't worry, Murray! He's nice.

Good boy, Murray! Good boy.

Murray?

Why don't you want to go
to the barbecue, Murray?

Don't worry, Murray!
There won't be any fireworks.

Good boy, Murray! Good boy.

Murray?

Why don't you want to go to bed, Murray?

Don't worry, Murray!
I'll stay right here with you
while you fall asleep.

Good boy, Murray!

You know, even though it wasn't easy,
you tried a lot of new things today.

And I'm proud of you.

Good night, Murray! My brave dog.